Twits on the Loose

A STEAMPUNK DISTRACTION

TOM ALAN ROBBINS

BOOK FOUR OF THE TWITS CHRONICLES

Claim A Free Gift!

Visit Twitschronicles.com to claim a free copy of the Twits short story *Uncle Hugo's Crisis"*. Or, if you are reading this on a device, you can click HERE.

What People Are Saying:

"The Twits Chronicles are hilarious, blessed with truly exceptional dialogue. Steampunk dystopia meets Oscar Wildean wit in these books. I found myself laughing out loud on numerous occasions--and that's not something I often do while reading. "

—Nick Sullivan, author of The Deep Series and Zombie Bigfoot.

"Delightful! A frothy frappe of P.G. Wodehouse and steam-punk. If you're the sort who reads blurbs before reading the book, stop it. Stop it right now. Read TWITS IN LOVE and have a good time. These days we can all use a bit more of a good time."

—John Ostrander, American writer of comic books, including *Suicide Squad, Grimjack* and *Star Wars: Legacy*.

"I haven't enjoyed the company of such eccentric characters since A Confederacy of Dunces, and Tom Alan Robbins has managed to place them in the stylized world of Oscar Wilde. A really unique journey."

— Kevin Conroy, Actor, The voice behind the DC Comics superhero Batman .

"Tom Alan Robbins' Twits stories are hilarious, thought provoking and mind bending. His juicy turns of phrase will stick in your ear like a catchy song."

— Michael Urie, Actor, Producer and Director

"Tom is the most talented, delicious writer. Do yourself a favor, and immerse yourself in the fabulous world of TWITS!"

— Mary Testa, 3 time Tony Award Nominee

The Author makes no representation of any kind as to his being a citizen of the United Kingdom, either native or naturalized. He is from a small town in Ohio, for which he apologizes.

This is a work of fiction. All events described are imaginary; all characters are entirely fictitious and are not intended to represent actual living persons.

Cover design by Melody J. Barber of Aurora Publicity

Additional designs by Eric Wright of The Puppet Kitchen.

Twits Logo designed by Feppa Rodriquez

Proofreading by Gretchen Tannert Douglas

For Nick Sullivan, who started me on this journey and who is still in the back seat with the map.

Steampunk

"Steampunk is a subgenre of science fiction that incorporates retrofuturistic technology and aesthetics inspired by 19th-century industrial steam-powered machinery. Steampunk works are often set in an alternative history of the Victorian era or the American "Wild West", where steam power remains in mainstream use, or in a fantasy world that similarly employs steam power."

Wikipedia

A Word About Timelines

For those who are unfamiliar with the Steampunk genre, a word about timelines may be helpful. The Steampunk Universe in which The Twits Chronicles take place is clearly not our own. That is why events and cultural references that happened in vastly different eras in our own world seem to happen in a compressed time period. It feels as if we are in a vaguely Victorian era, and yet there are references to events and quotations from well into the twentieth century.

It may help to think of this as an exercise in "what if?" What if electricity wasn't discovered until much later in human history? Human ingenuity would still search for new ways of using existing technology, and so steam power and mechanical engineering would keep advancing, while much of the aesthetic of the world around us could remain in the nineteenth century.

The world that would result is the world of *The Twits Chronicles*. Other writers would use these same criteria to create very different realities. This is mine.

Enter and enjoy.

Contents

Foreword

Heigh-ho! Cyril Chippington-Smythe here. Perhaps you have heard the name bandied about at my good old club, Twits. The general opinion of me at the Club is that I am a scream. As Badger Binghampton put it, "The good lord put you on this earth to lighten the mood, Cyril and there is no occasion so bleak that you can't draw a laugh with one of your farcical attempts at coherent thought." Very kind of him I'm sure, but I just say whatever pops into my head with no attempt to shape it beyond tossing a noun and a verb into the flow now and then.

No one was more surprised than I to learn that my mechanical valet, Bentley, has been recording my utterances and chronicling my adventures for years. He states that his records are more for purposes of legal defense than entertainment, but I showed them around to the fellows and they insisted that I have them published. I am told that their length qualifies them as "novellas", which I always thought was a kind of pasta.

If you are a follower of these Chronicles, you know that my chinless cousin Binky is a blister of the first water when it comes to romance. He has a genius for falling head over heels in love with the most inexplicable of potential partners. The usual plot requires me to move Heaven and Earth to ensure the success of his suit and then to lug them painfully back to their original locations to get him out of the soup. This latest episode is an especially virulent example in which Bentley is forced to overlook some pretty petty behavior on my part in order to come to the rescue.

Off you go, then. Perhaps you should place a platter of crackers and a cup of tea within easy reach to stave off hunger and thirst. Bentley's chronicles can be gripping. Consider yourself warned!

CHAPTER ONE

I'm Only a Bird in a Gilded Cage

Great wealth is like an ill-tempered dog. One hopes for a frolicsome companion and finds instead the teeth of responsibility locked onto one's ankle. I had recently come of age and the weight of my family's fortune had transformed me from a witty and attractive boulevardier into a hollow shell who slumped over his brandy and Paxil beweeping his outcast state. Playing cards even for astronomical sums brought no flush to my cheeks. What is money when there is an endless supply of it? Friends who had always slapped one on the back and shared a scandalous tale now grew silent at my approach or tried awkwardly to touch me for a tenner to pay the bar tab. Slowly all of my acquaintance drifted away. All but my cousin, Cheswick Wickford-Davies (Binky to his friends). Years of sponging had left him with no sense of shame. Hence, he was immune to the corrupting influence of wealth.

It was a gloomy morning in April when my mechanical valet, Bentley, wafted into the parlour bearing a medicinal dose of something distilled by monks in the Pyrenees and the news that Binky was champing at the bit to see me.

"Show him in, Bentley. Mr. Wickford-Davies has the run of the keep at all times."

"Very good, Sir."

Bentley floated off in that way he has and returned with Binky moping behind him.

"Hallo, Old Sausage! Live free or die," chirped I.

"What?"

"That's the new thing. 'Live free or die.' I had it from Bentley this morning."

"Not 'Confusion to our enemies'?"

I flapped a flipper breezily. "No, that's old news."

He fell heavily into a chair and rubbed his face with his hands. "Why do these mottoes always feature death so prominently?"

"I suppose because thoughts of mortality cause one to reflect. These are national slogans, you know—not advertisements for soap flakes."

"May I point out that the Sudso soap flakes ad features plague, pestilence and flesh-eating organisms in its jingle? I think rhyming 'hysteria' with 'bacteria' is awfully good." He subsided back into melancholia.

"Was there a reason you invaded the family domicile this morning?"

He ran his fingers through his hair and groaned. "I've come to the end, Cyril. Life is a hollow shell."

I had heard this sort of thing from him too many times to be very alarmed. "Bentley? Suggestions?"

Bentley gave a judicious little nod. "Perhaps an ounce of tequila and a serotonin reuptake inhibitor?"

"Good! On the double, before he sinks into an existential fugue. These things are contagious, you know."

"At once, Sir."

Bentley disapparated like a soap bubble and I examined the patient. "Out with it, Old Shoe. What's got you howling at the moon?"

He gave out with another shivering groan and stared at the ceiling. "There's this girl, you see..."

Well, that was all I needed to hear. This was more or less a weekly occurrence and my patience was threadbare. "Honestly, you'd fall in love with a shovel if there was nothing else handy."

He stared at me with bloodshot eyes. "She looks right through me."

"Myopic, is she? You're rather hard to miss. Beefy, what?"

This seemed to wound him. "I've never been so thin."

"Oh, absolutely. Nearly transparent."

"I'm too miserable to eat."

Bentley shimmered into view, holding a glass of tequila and a pill on a tray. Binky took them both and downed the pill gratefully.

"Will there be anything else, Sir?"

"Nothing, Bentley, thank you."

And he was gone, just like that. Bentley could have had a brilliant career as a magician, but of course fame means nothing to a steam-powered domestic.

"Drink your tequila like a good lad. Why does your lady love treat you so spuriously?"

He slumped and sipped his drink. "It's my own fault. I have no character to speak of and she's so...

good. She's given away her entire fortune to assist the downtrodden... positively destitute now."

"She sounds gruesome, if you don't mind my saying so."

"You haven't met her. One is quite helpless before the torrent of her animal spirits. She attracts more followers every day."

"Really? Who's after her—detectives, creditors?"

"Spiritual followers. People who look to her for guidance."

"She doesn't sound like your usual poison. You've always been drawn to girls who enjoy a good rugby match and that sort of thing."

Before I could enquire further, Bentley entered the room and it is some indication of his mental agitation that I saw him coming quite clearly from the top of the stairs. The look on his face was as close to horror as the materials it was constructed of would allow.

"I beg your pardon, Sir. Did you order a... TV?"

"Is it here already? That's fast work."

He looked at me as I'm sure Samson looked at Delilah after his haircut. "There were two persons at the front door. I sent them away."

What ho, this was a little high-handed! Bentley is normally as servile as one would wish a mechanical valet to be, but every now and then he takes the bit in his teeth. "Sent them away? By what right?"

He gazed at me for a moment and I heard his gears grinding away. "A TV is... unsuitable, Sir."

Bentley tossed out the word "unsuitable" the way prisoners hurl their slops during a prison riot, but a chap has to stand up for himself now and then if he is not to become a supernumerary in his own home.

"That's hardly up to you, is it? If I want a bally TV I'll have a bally TV. Who is the employer here, you or I?"

"You, Sir," he admitted... rather reluctantly, I thought.

"You run that couple down and bring them up here at once. That's an order."

There was a further grinding of gears. "Yes, Sir."

Bentley's accustomed pace is a dignified glide, but when the occasion calls for it, he has legs like pistons. Indeed, his legs *are* pistons. He was out the front door like a shot and in a few moments, I heard him climbing the stairs followed by a rather flashily dressed lady and gentleman carrying large cases. He gestured to them and all but sneered.

"Your TV, Sir."

The gentleman hefted his case and looked around. "Good morning, Sir. Where shall we set up?"

"I hadn't really thought about it."

The lady staggered a bit under the weight of her cases. "What room do you frequent most?"

I thought for a moment. "The bedroom, I suppose."

She frowned. "We can't recommend the bedroom, Sir. Too stimulating."

"Oh, then I suppose... here."

"Very good. Just give us a minute."

There was a flurry of activity as they disposed of their cases by the wall and did some quick stretching exercises. Adjusting their clothing, they stepped to the center of the room and cleared their throats. The gentleman began. "All right Sir, here we go. I'm Smith."

"And I'm Jones."

"And we are..."

"Thought Vacation!"

"World got you down? Portents of death and decay ruining your fun?"

"Lean back and let us take you on a Thought Vacation!"

The lady had a little clown horn with a rubber bulb which she honked a couple of times.

Binky jiggled on his toes. "Oh, I say, What fun!"

"It *is* fun, Sir. What would you like to see?"

I stepped forth eagerly. "What are my choices?"

"Oh, anything. We can do comedy, drama, news and weather, sports, game shows—you name it."

Binky gave a little titter. "Where on earth did you find them?"

"Cheeseworth put me on to them. TV is the latest thing. What shall we watch?"

He thought for moment. "Comedy?"

"All right." I turned to the pair. "Comedy, then."

The gentleman stepped to a case and began to snap it open. "Very good. Let me just get out our custard pies and inflated pig's bladder."

"No, it's too much bother. What about some drama?"

Now the lady ran to another case. "Of course, Sir. Where did I put that pistol? Do you mind loud noises, Sir?"

I waved her off. "What can you do without props?"

The gentleman thought for a moment. "Sports? We can do bare-fisted boxing, wrestling, the long jump and for an extra fee we can acquire a ping-pong table."

The lady clasped her hands together and looked at me imploringly. "Please, Sir, not boxing. My bruises haven't healed from our last engagement."

Smith growled at her. "Don't whine. I've told you to protect the body."

"Just the news. That doesn't require props, does it?" I asked.

"No, Sir. News it is."

The gentleman stood center and cleared his throat. He stared off into the middle distance. "The standoff continues at the Vatican. The Pope still declares that she will not wear the traditional robes and mitre because, as she puts it, 'I wouldn't wear that outfit to a hootenanny.' The College of Cardinals is taking the position that if they can wear the robe and mitre in the heat of a Roman Summer then the Pope can do so as well and if she doesn't like it she can lump it. When reminded that the Pope is infallible, they replied that infallibility only applies to dogma and not fashion."

I turned to Binky. "What do you think, Old Boy?"

"In local news..."

I waved at the gentleman, who was plowing ahead. "I say, you can stop for a moment."

He looked at me with disappointment. "You should say, 'Off,' Sir."

"I see. There's a protocol."

"Yes, Sir. Off, on, faster, louder, funnier... that sort of thing."

"Very well... off."

The pair backed up and stood next to their cases. The lady raised her hand. "Before we sign off may we just say that Bunbury's Lotion gives your skin that melasma-free glow that the ladies adore."

The two entertainers lost all animation and stood on the carpet rather self-consciously. Smith gave a little cough. Binky looked at me nervously.

"Well now they're just staring at us."

I addressed the pair. "Do you mean that when you're 'Off' you just stand there all day doing nothing?"

Smith shrugged. "Ours is not an easy life."

"Can't you go for a walk?"

He looked at me sadly. "Show business, Sir."

We stood for a moment watching them watch us.

"It's rather disconcerting," Binky observed.

"I quite agree."

"Should we go somewhere else?"

"Yes! Let's step into the bedroom. They won't follow us there."

"No Sir, that costs extra," Jones quickly agreed.

"We'll be here when you want us, Sir."

"Thought Vacation, at your service."

Binky and I practically ran through the bedroom door and slammed it behind us. I could hear the muffled sounds of an argument breaking out.

I gave the door a worried look. "I say, perhaps this TV thingamabob isn't all it's cracked up to be."

Binky shrugged. "Send it back."

"And give Bentley the moral advantage? Impossible. One must simply bear it."

He looked at me enviously. "How I wish I had your strength of character."

"Alas, Nature does not distribute her gifts equally." I sat down on the bed. "Now, what are you going to do about your lady love?"

His spirits, which had risen with the excitement of the TV, came crashing down. He began to pace between the dresser and the wardrobe. "What can I do? I have nothing to offer her. I have no moral compass, no character and no money."

"Money is vastly overrated. I have scads of cash and it has brought nothing but misery. There are mornings I can barely get out of bed. Sometimes I wish... but there it is... I'm stuck with it."

"We're a couple of sad cases... you destroyed by wealth and I by unrequited love."

"Nothing to be done, I'm afraid. We must simply bear it."

"I say, do you suppose Bentley has any helpful suggestions? He's always come through in the past."

I perked up at once. "An excellent idea. Bentley?"

I don't believe he opened the door. He was merely there in the room. "Did you wish me to return the TV, Sir?

There was a hint of smugness in his voice, which I hastened to quash. "Absolutely not! Best purchase in ages. Riotous fun! Wouldn't part with it for anything. Thinking of getting one for the guest room."

He raised an eyebrow. "I see."

"No, we called to ask for your advice."

"Indeed?"

"It seems that our friend Binky here has tumbled head over heels for a young lady who is on too high a moral plane to spot him crawling in the dust beneath her."

He turned his optical sensors on Binky. "May I ask the young lady's name, Sir?"

"Anjelica De Souza-Kleinhoffer," said Binky reverently.

"Ever heard of her?"

"Yes, Sir. She presents herself as a spiritual guide."

"That's the one."

"Is that all, Sir?"

"Well, actually... no. As long as we're plotting I've been meaning to ask you if you can think of a way for me to oil out from under the weight of all these riches. It's become deucedly uncomfortable. The chaps at the club have gotten rather standoffish and one feels like a pariah."

Binky rubbed my shoulder sympathetically. "Poor old Cyril. He's being positively crushed, Bentley."

"Wealth is a millstone, I tell you—a golden millstone around my neck."

Bentley turned his face to the ceiling and gave the plaster a good inspection. "Is there any other pertinent information, Sir?"

"No, I think that's all."

He stood still for moment and his gears ground away merrily.

Binky regarded him eagerly. "What's the plan, Bentley?"

He tore his gaze from the ceiling and seemed surprised to find us still standing there. "Nothing, Sir."

Bentley is usually the first to jump in with a suggestion or two. This sudden reticence was baffling.

"Nothing will come from nothing. Speak again," I said.

"I'm afraid that no solution presents itself at the present time."

"What? You always save the day. Is it a mechanical problem?"

"I am in perfect working order, Sir."

"And you have no suggestions?"

"I'm afraid not, Sir."

Suddenly I knew what had happened. He was miffed about the TV. One would think that his programming would force him to be helpful, but there's always some way to weasel around those things. Bentley's brain was a complicated piece of machinery and had apparently developed the ability to have a snit. I eyed him coldly. "I see. You may go."

"Very good, Sir."

He deliberately paced to the door, opened it and strode out with no attempt to glide or shimmer in any way. Binky stared after him.

"That was odd."

"Yes. I'm afraid we're on our own."

He looked at me thoughtfully. "Well, look here, I've got an idea about your excess of filthy lucre."

"Have you? Out with it, Old Sponge."

"Why don't you give it away?"

"Steady on. One doesn't just give away the family fortune will you nill you."

"Why not?"

"There's logistics... tax considerations... not to mention that my Aunt Hypatia would make the mythological Harpies look like parakeets."

He thought for a moment. "Well, you could just... *tell* people you'd given it away. A *'ruse de guerre'* as it were."

"You mean a lie."

"Well... yes."

"What reason would I give?"

"Tell them the truth. It was too much trouble."

I shook my head. "It sounds weak, Old Brisket. They'd never swallow it."

Binky was growing more feverish by the moment. Having ideas made the blood rush to his head and he was apt to suddenly faint and pitch into the nearest fireplace. I readied myself to catch him.

"I have it! Tell them you lost it to me in a bet!" he said.

"What?"

"Say we bet on something. You know—we'd been drinking and you said, 'I'll bet my whole fortune that ant gets to your eclair before that other ant,' and I said, 'You're on,' and I won."

"Will they believe it?"

"We've done more improbable things than that."

I smiled bitterly. "Buying that circus was a case in point."

"They swore they had an elephant. It would have been a gold mine!"

"But they never actually specified it was alive. The smell haunts me to this day."

"Let's not cry over spilt elephants."

"Or spoilt elephants in this case. So the story will be that you're rich and I'm poor?"

"You'll have the onus of great wealth removed from you and I shall be elevated by the rumor of that same wealth to a plane that makes me visible to my lady love."

"I thought she didn't care about money."

"People who say that spend an awful lot of time with rich people. Once I've got her attention I know I can win her over."

I looked at it from every angle and could find no flaw. "By Jove, it makes a Byzantine kind of sense."

"Should we run it by Bentley?"

I drew myself up icily. "What for? It's a perfect plan."

Binky hugged himself. "Someone must have walked on my grave. I got a shiver."

"I'm not going to give him a chance to poo-poo it. He's quite puffed up enough as it is. He needs to see that he's not indispensable."

"Why don't we toddle over to the club and start the rumor mill churning? If Cheeseworth is there, the word will be all over town by teatime."

We started for the door but I jerked to a stop. "Drat. We'll have to pass by the TV on the way out."

Binky eyed the door nervously. "No way around them?"

"Not unless we crawl out the window. Just keep your eyes forward and don't acknowledge them."

"Off we go, then."

I threw back what pass for my shoulders and bowled through the door. The TV came to life with a roar.

"Welcome back, Sir. Care for a bit of fun?"

"Juicy political scandal, Sir."

"Oh! I've torn my bodice. Please don't look!"

"Off! Off!" I cried. "Damn your eyes, off!"

Smith wrung his hands piteously. "Any chance of lunch, Sir?"

I didn't stop to reply. As we rounded a corner, Jones called after us... "Remember—Chatterly's pink pills will keep your impacted colon smooth and lubricated. Available at a pharmacy near you."

We slowed to a walk.

"That was terrifying," panted Binky.

"I suppose one gets used to it."

"It provides a sort of company, I suppose. You could never be lonely."

"But the constant, desperate need for one's attention makes it impossible to think."

"How much time do you really spend thinking in a typical day, though? I'm guessing no more than five or ten minutes."

I eyed him frostily. "Those are precious minutes. I will not surrender them."

"Good luck, then. Shall I drive us to the club?"

There was a time when I delighted in outrageous and luxurious vehicles, but experience had shown me the hubris of such overenthusiastic transportation and at the moment I was taking taxis whenever I needed to get somewhere. Binky, however, felt no such compunction.

"What are you riding in these days?"

"Dogsled. Eight huskies."

I whistled. "Rather opulent."

"Oh no. I got it used. The dogs are a little threadbare. Some have lost all their teeth. It gets me where I'm going, though. Shotgun..."

"You don't have to call shotgun when it's just the two of us."

"No, I brought a shotgun. It's in the sled. There's been a bit of trouble with the protests."

We reached the street and there, before us, was the aforementioned dogsled. The robotic huskies woofed and snarled in their traces. Binky tossed a heavy fur coat in my direction.

"Here. Put on this Anorak and these Mukluks."

"I beg your pardon?"

"Verisimilitude. One can't ride down the street in a dogsled wearing a morning jacket. It spoils the illusion."

"But it's eighty degrees!"

"Fashion makes no allowance for comfort."

I struggled into the steaming mound. "I won't wear the gloves."

"Fine. Just keep your hands in your pockets. Now, I'll just enter our destination. Drat. How do you spell 'Twits'?"

"Sound it out. T, Tw, Twi..."

"Don't confuse me."

I looked at him in astonishment. "Can you not read?"

"I'm just a little rusty. My valet reads everything to me."

"Here, let me do it."

I tapped in the address and the dogs began to jump and bark.

"That's got it. Hop on the runner and hold on for dear life."

Binky reached over toward the cargo bin.

"Let me just get my shotg..."

There was a loud "bang!" and one of the mechanical hounds fell silent.

"Well, now it's a seven-dog sled. Put the safety on, for all love."

He hung his head. "Sorry."

"Yoiks! And away!"

As we raced through the streets, I felt almost... hopeful. Soon my friends would gaze upon me with the pity I once enjoyed and commiserate on my new found, if illusory, poverty. The pity was certainly in my future, but not for the reasons I imagined. I little suspected that these hounds of hell were drawing me inexorably to my doom.

CHAPTER TWO

Hoist by My Own Petard

It has been said that if you know a man's club, you know the man. Twits, the club of the Chippington-Smythes since man discovered fire, was a case in point. Rigid? Yes. But underneath its brass and Naugahyde there was an undeniable spirit of fun—cards, gossip, roulette, amateur theatricals—all bathed in a constant stream of alcohol.

I saw that the crowd of protesters outside the club was noticeably larger. The most prominent of the signs demanded: "Stop Defining Me with Your Expectations!"

"What on earth does that mean?"

Binky grinned. "It's one of Anjelica's pet peeves. I told you she had followers."

"She seems rather esoteric in her thinking. How do you keep up?"

A blush crept into his cheeks. "We communicate on a more physical plane."

I hurried up the steps and Binky slouched behind me with his firearm.

Evans, the club's eternal doorman, greeted Binky and me at the entrance. "Good morning, gentlemen. May I take your shotgun?"

Binky handed it over. "Thank you, Evans."

"I'll just remove the shells, if I may."

He cocked the shotgun loudly and ejected the shells. He frowned at them. "One of the shells has been fired."

"An accident, Evans. Binky performed an unintentional *coup de grace* on one of his mechanical sled dogs."

"I see, Sir. Very droll."

I looked around to confirm that we couldn't be overheard. "Evans, anything we tell you is privileged information, yes? You are bound to take it with you to the grave?"

He bowed his head. "Alas, servants such as I are denied the sweet release of death."

"It's only an expression, Evans."

"Of course, Sir, but one does tend to brood after two or three centuries. I am bound by the laws of confidentiality embedded in my code. I am unable to reveal anything that is told to me in private."

"That's fine. Mr. Wickford-Davies and I are pulling a little prank. The story is that I lost all of my money to him in a bet. He's the rich one now and I haven't got a penny to my name."

There was a release of steam from the corner of his mouth that sounded suspiciously like a sigh. "I see, Sir. Most amusing."

"Can you arrange it with the club treasurer to let Binky here sign for things and charge it to my account? In essence, as far as finances go, he will be me. Does that convey the gist?"

"Yes, Sir. I will arrange it at once. Just sign here."

He produced a document and a pen. I scribbled my name and the thing was done. Binky stared at the paper thoughtfully.

"I can sign for anything?"

"Yes, Sir."

"And Cyril pays for it?"

"Exactly, Sir."

He looked wonderingly around the room. "It's like a dream I once had, but in the dream I could fly."

I spotted C. Langford-Cheeseworth lounging on the other side of the lobby. He was patting a mound of fleecy curls that upon closer inspection turned out to be a young man wearing what seemed to be a sheep costume.

I nudged Binky. "There's Cheeseworth. Time to put our plan into motion."

Cheeseworth waved languidly. "Yoo-hoo! Cywil! Binky! Live fwee or die."

"Live free or die."

"Live free or die. I say, Cheeseworth, I'm a little baffled by this lamb-like companion of yours."

"It's the latest thing. He's a pet, you see. I went him by the day. His name is Compton. Say hello, Compton."

The fleecy creature peered up at me from underneath its lamb headpiece.

"Hello, Sirs. Baa. I believe you're standing on my tail."

"Sorry. Pleasure to meet you, Compton."

Cheeseworth held out a bundle of grass. "Here, you can feed him."

Compton's eyes grew moist. "Please, Sir, not more grass. It gives me the runs something terrible. Baa."

Cheeseworth glared at his woolly companion. "Stop whining. The wental agweement doesn't require me to feed you at all. Count your blessings."

"Baa. Thank you, Sir. Very grateful I'm sure."

Cheeseworth turned back to us. "Are you lunching?"

I assumed a humble demeanor. "Well, the sad truth is, I can't afford it. Unless Binky here treats me."

Binky waved expansively. "Oh! Please be my guest. Order anything you like. The sky's the limit."

"I'm quite bewildered. What does this sudden weversal of fortune portend?"

I looked around and leaned in conspiratorially. "Can you keep a secret?"

"I don't know. I've never twied."

"There is wailing and gnashing of teeth at the house of Chippington-Smythe today. I have put a blot on the family escutcheon. I've lost everything to Binky here on a wager."

His eyes grew large. "What was the bet?"

Binky hopped in. "Well! We were in the sitting room... sitting, you know, and I had a cinnamon bun..."

I tried to catch his eye. "I thought it was an eclair."

"I don't like eclairs."

"Just trying to stay consistent, you know."

"Who's telling this story?"

"Oh, you! By all means."

Cheeseworth's head had been bobbing back and forth. "Is the vawiety of pastwy important to the nawative?"

"No! It was a cinnamon bun, and there were two giant cockroaches eyeing it."

I glared at him. "Don't tell people my house is infested with cockroaches. It's hard enough to get anyone to come to tea."

Cheeseworth gave Compton's head a pat. "I don't mind cockwoaches at all. I had one as a pet in leaner times." His eyes grew misty. "I named him 'Sandwich'... because I found him in my sandwich."

Binky plowed ahead. "So! These two great, slimy cockroaches were eyeing my bun and I said to Cyril, 'I'll bet you that brown one on the left gets to the bun first,' and Cyril said, 'I'll wager my entire fortune that the beefy bruiser on the right takes the prize.' I said, 'Done,' and with that my roach took off as if he'd only been waiting for us to close the deal. He'd burrowed halfway through my cinnamon bun before the other one had left the gate."

Cheeseworth's mouth hung open. "And now you're wich and Cyril is a pauper? It wivals the worst excesses of Dickens."

I hung my head in shame. "Keep it to yourself, will you Cheeseworth? I couldn't bear the humiliation."

He patted my hand. "Now, now. Shame is a very attwactive quality in a man. It suffuses everyone awound him with the warm glow of self-satisfaction."

I frowned at him. "By the by, that TV you put me onto is a pestilence. What were you thinking?"

"Yes, it requires far too much maintenance. I went to the countwy and forgot to put out food and water. I came back to find the TV gasping on the carpet in the last thwoes of dehydwation. I put it out on the curb on twash collection day and by midmorning it was gone. When last heard from it, it was entertaining at a pub in Ipswich."

"Have you lunched, Cheeseworth?" asked Binky.

"I never lunch. It makes me bilious. I have a dwy husk at ten and then nothing until dinner."

"Well, we're going in."

"*Bonne chance*. I hear the soup today has an almost wecognizable flavour."

I nodded at him. "Thanks. We'll try it. Now remember, my lowly financial status is a dark secret."

"I am a sealed cwypt. Enjoy your lunch."

We strolled into the dining room to find Rodgers, the maître d', at his accustomed post. "Good afternoon, gentlemen. Table for two?"

"Yes, thank you Rodgers. Has Evans apprised you of our financial arrangement?"

He lowered his voice. "Yes, Sir. All of Mr. Wickford-Davies charges will be deducted from your account."

Binky clapped his hands. "Goodie!"

"This way, gentlemen."

As we approached our table, I spied my Uncle Hugo reading the paper and cramming bread into his mouth. I tried to slide behind a palm plant but he had spotted me.

"Cyril!"

"Uncle Hugo! What a surprise."

"Confusion to our enemies."

I smiled indulgently. "I'm afraid that's expired, Uncle. It's 'Live free or die' now."

"Is it?" He looked nonplussed. "Is the implication that suicide is preferable to government regulation?"

"I haven't really thought about it."

He considered for a moment then shook his head. "No, these slogans seldom make any logical sense. The real point is uniformity of outlook. I was hoping to run into you. Your aunt wishes you to come for the weekend."

This was grim news. "To Dankworth Hall?"

"Yes."

I assumed a look of angelic innocence. My voice rose an octave. "Tomorrow?"

"Yes."

"Oh... what a shame..."

"I will stop you there. She will brook no refusal. If you have other plans, you must cancel them."

"I say."

"You know your aunt."

"Only too well. May I bring Binky?"

"Certainly. I believe an acquaintance of his will be in attendance. A Ms. Anjelica De Souza-Kleinhoffer."

Binky snapped to attention at the mention of her name. "Anjelica! She'll be there?"

"Mrs. Dankworth is quite fascinated by her. If I didn't know Hypatia's strength of character I might be concerned."

Rodgers paced among the diners with his gong. "We are each responsible for our own happiness.

We can choose to have new responses to old stimuli."

Gong!

"Happiness is surmounting not unknowable obstacles in order to achieve knowable goals."

I waved him over. "I say, Rodgers, what are these mysterious pronouncements? What's happened to the news of the world?"

He gave a little bow. "We have sub-contracted the content of our dining room presentations to Ms. De Souza-Kleinhoffer's Institute, Sir."

Binky grinned. "I thought they sounded familiar."

"Rather opaque, aren't they?"

"We have been instructed to respond to that criticism with, 'To achieve greater understanding, attend one of our seminars for a nominal fee. See the concierge for details.'"

"I see. Carry on, then."

He stepped away and gave his gong a good thumping. "Thinkingness is the study of thinking. The enemy of thinkingness is knowingness."

A voice spun me around. "Cyril, Old Bean! Where've you been hiding?"

My old friend, Ford, was wobbling toward me on a pair of sequined platforms. His inevitable consort, Lincoln, picked his way carefully behind him. These two dissolute companions of my youth were among those whose shoulders had cooled toward me.

"Hallo, Ford. Hallo, Lincoln... nowhere special. Live free or die."

"Live free or die."

"Live free or die."

Ford gave my shoulder a good pounding. "You've been avoiding your friends."

Lincoln worked the midsection. "Very naughty."

Ford massaged my scalp with his knuckles. "We must do dinner! What about getting the gang together next week for drinks at that new workingman's pub."

Lincoln thumped me soundly in the chest. "It's too divine. You drink with the masses."

Binky had been bobbing his head and chuckling at the jibes. "Am I invited too?"

Ford looked at him rather coolly. "Won't you be dining at some frightfully expensive place?"

"This is rather low class for a patrician like you, Old Midas."

Binky's eyes reddened a bit. "Oh, I say..."

Cheeseworth had clearly been hard at work. News of our financial reversal had spread and my long-lost friends were once again clasping me to their collective bosoms. I returned their affectionate punches vigorously, managing to connect with a jab to Lincoln's nose.

"I'd love to come. It's been ages."

Ford smacked a kindly hand on my shoulder. "And listen, my lad, it will be my treat. I won't take no for an answer."

"Rather!"

At that moment I saw the club's beady-eyed marshall, Cubby Martinez, striding toward us. Cubby is generally held to be a blister of exceptional size and virulence.

"Morning Cubby. You look rather grim, I must say."

"Official business, I'm afraid. Mr. Chippington-Smythe, may I have a word with you in private?"

I smiled graciously. "You can speak freely. These are my friends and relations."

"Don't make this harder than it has to be."

Ford and Lincoln were eyeing Cubby distastefully. "We've got to skedaddle anyway."

"See you next week, Old Boy. Looking forward to it."

They tripped away.

"Look here, Cubby, we haven't even ordered yet. I'll come by your office after lunch."

Cubby smiled, which revealed a rather yellow set of teeth. "I'm afraid you won't be eating lunch, Chippington-Smythe."

"Botulism in the kitchen again?"

"The dining room is for members only..."

"I certainly hope so."

His smile grew wider and more malevolent. "And your membership has been suspended."

Uncle Hugo rose up on his hind paws to defend the family honor. "On whose authority?"

"The club treasurer, Sir. I'm afraid Mr. Chippington-Smythe no longer meets the minimum financial requirements for membership."

My uncle stared at him, dumbfounded. "My nephew is one of the richest men in the world!"

"Not any more, Sir."

"What?"

"Word has reached us that he is destitute."

My uncle whirled toward me. "Cyril! Explain yourself!"

"Now, Uncle, it's a misunderstanding."

Cubby was grinning outright now. "Did you or did you not lose the entirety of your fortune to Mr. Wickford-Davies here on a wager involving insects?"

Binky raised a finger. "He did! I can buy and sell the lot of you now if I like."

My uncle grew apoplectic. "Is this true?"

"Uncle, could I speak to you outside?"

"No! Answer me this minute! Is this unbelievable story true?"

You see my dilemma. Binky and I had launched our perfect plan and it was working like gangbusters. To explode it now would expose us to ridicule without accomplishing any of our aims. This is the place where Bentley usually popped in and made some pithy observation that put everything right, but he was a no-show. I saw no other options.

"It is true in a sense, but there is more to the story than meets the eye. If I could just..."

My uncle was the colour of what I had recently learned were called 'beets.' "By God, Sir! In my day you would have been tarred and feathered!"

Hurling his napkin to the floor he headed for the exit. He paused to shoot a parting barb in my direction. "Your aunt will have something to say to you and I do not envy you the experience."

I waved weakly at his departing back. "Ta! Until the weekend. Looking forward to it."

Cubby stepped forward smoothly and reached for my arm. "May I escort you out?"

I shook off his hand. "I can see myself out, thank you. Come on, Binky."

He looked at the table guiltily. *"I'm* still a member."

I stared at him, aghast. "You're not going to sit here and eat lunch without me?"

"I'm hungry."

"Well... really!"

It was a sadly chastened Cyril Chippington-Smythe that staggered home to lick his wounds. I moped into the parlour, forgetting the horror that lay in wait.

"Welcome back, Sir!"

"Just in time for comedy!"

There was the honk of a clown horn.

"Bentley, some assistance!" I bellowed.

Jones adopted an exaggerated pose, with hands on hips. She waggled her eyebrows at Smith. "Who was that lady I saw you with?"

"That was no lady. That was an autonomous steam-powered sex robot to whom I am affianced."

Jones grabbed a drumstick and smacked a nearby cymbal.

"A protester came up to me the other day and said, 'Hey mister, can you help me? I haven't had a bite in three days.'"

"What did you do?"

"I bit him... and got hepatitis."

Another crash.

"Bentley! Where the deuce are you?" I croaked.

At last, he oozed through the doorway. "Here, Sir."

"What took you so long?"

"I was in the cellar, Sir, rotating the claret."

Smith and Jones had paused to observe this interchange, but at the first pause in the conversational flow they leapt back into animation.

"I broke my arm in two places."

"What did the doctor say?"

"Stay out of those places! They're clearly full of disaffected anarchists."

Crash!

"Off! Off!" I cried, waving my arms.

Smith looked at me mournfully. "We can be funnier, Sir. It's just that we're so terribly hungry."

"Bentley, can you give them something to eat?"

He shook his head disapprovingly and sighed. "If you wish it, Sir."

"We can't very well let them starve."

Jones wiped a little drool from the corner of his mouth and raised a hand. "When hunger strikes, strike back with Uncle Cuthbert's genuine lamby and onionlike stew. Now with more lamby flavour." His voice dropped to a whisper. "Lamb and onions not included."

"Quickly, Bentley! Into the bedroom."

I practically ran to the safety of my sleeping chamber. Bentley glided in after me and gazed at me with exaggerated sympathy. "Shall I return the TV, Sir?"

I drew myself up haughtily. "What? And miss all that hilarious comedy?"

He raised an eyebrow. "They seemed to upset you."

"Not at all. It's just... I didn't want to miss the finer points of their performance. I'll go back when I'm rested and really dig into all that content."

He gave a little sniff and began folding handkerchiefs. "How was your visit to the club, Sir?"

I eyed him nervously. "Oh, the usual."

"You came back rather quickly."

"It was pretty dead. Didn't see the point of staying."

He turned to me with a face empty of expression. "Mr. Martinez sent a message."

"Damn his beady little eyes!"

"I was instructed to remove the club crest from all relevant apparel."

I fell onto the bed. "Oh, Bentley, it's too humiliating. To be escorted from one's club like a common... person."

He cocked his head to the side. "Am I to understand that your fortune is now in the hands of Mr. Wickford-Davies?"

"No! It was a *ruse de guerre*!"

"A lie, Sir?"

"Well... yes."

"I am relieved to hear it."

I proceeded to explain the whole sordid affair to Bentley, who absorbed it in silence—only his optical sensors flicking back and forth to indicate his mental activity. When I had finished, he stood for a moment and then reached out to straighten an errant lamp shade.

"What do you think of all I've told you?"

"I really couldn't say, Sir."

I stared at him, dumbfounded. "Don't you have any thoughts?"

"Not at the present time, Sir."

I am not ashamed to admit to a bit of a lump in the old throat. "Dash it all, I poured out my soul to you."

"Most gratifying, Sir. One feels quite unworthy."

I knew Bentley was miffed about the TV but this was an emergency! One expects the troops to rally 'round. Apparently, I had misjudged our relationship. We were, after all, nothing but master and servant. I assumed a chilly demeanor.

"We are leaving for Dankworth Hall in the morning. Pack the usual accouterments."

"Very good, Sir."

And with that he was gone. I sat grimly, listening to the TV grumbling and coughing in the next room. I felt a bit like that Lear chap, if he'd had an ungrateful child made out of metal. I reflected on how sharper than a serpent's tooth it is to have a thankless valet and tried to squeeze out a tear or two with no success. Tomorrow I would face my Aunt Hypatia, with famine, sword and fire leashed in at her heels like hounds and no Bentley to stand as my bulwark. I feared it would be a day to try the sinews of the heir to the house of Chippington-Smythe.

CHAPTER THREE

The Guru Was a Lady

Binky had offered to transport Bentley and myself to Dankworth Hall and so, at an hour early enough to dismay the morning lark, we trundled out to the curb. There was still a frostiness between us as we waited on the pavement. I cast about for something to break the ice.

"A bit chilly, what?"

"Yes, Sir."

I tried again.

"I say, what was all that commotion with the TV this morning?"

"They objected to being chained to the radiator, Sir."

I stared at Bentley. "Was that necessary?"

"I thought it prudent."

"But they'll starve, won't they?"

"I left a package of rolls and the chains permit them to reach the sink in the pantry."

I thought for a moment. "What about the bathroom?"

"There is a bucket, Sir."

"That's all right then." I shot him a look out of the corner of my eye. "Shame if anything were to happen to that TV. I'm terribly keen on it."

"So you have said, Sir."

At that moment a vision out of Hieronymus Bosch rounded the corner, with Binky sitting behind the wheel.

He waved gaily. "Hallo!"

"What on earth?"

As it grew nearer one could see that it was an enormous swan boat, easily thirty feet long. The giant swan leered down at us with an expression of mingled derision and longing.

"What's this? Where's the dogsled?"

"I gave it away! Splurged on something a little more fitting. Do you like it? It's amphibious."

"How ever could you afford it?"

"Oh, I charged it to you. I used your account at the club."

My mouth opened and closed a few times. "But..."

"I have to keep up appearances. I'm supposed to be the rich one, remember?"

"Couldn't you find something a little more modest?"

"In for a penny, in for a pound."

"I have no idea what that means."

"Hop in back, Bentley. Cyril, you crawl in next to me. Mind the feathers."

I did my best to navigate through the plumage and into the front seat. Binky cranked the gear shaft. The swan let out a huge 'Honk!' and we began to lurch forward.

"Hold on. It tends to wobble a bit. Not very aerodynamic, I'm afraid."

Binky is a terrible driver under the best of circumstances and a swan boat is not built for high-speed travel. We lost our feathery crest at the first underpass and it was downhill from there. Still, we glided up to the front door of Dankworth Hall more or less intact. Mrs. Pine, the housekeeper, awaited us. She was a model identical to my own housekeeper, Mrs. Oakes.

"Good morning, gentlemen. Mrs. Dankworth is awaiting you in the morning room."

"Thank you, Mrs. Pine."

Binky seized my arm and whispered hoarsely into my ear.

"Now remember, you mustn't explode our story. You've got your half—everyone thinks you're poor and pities you extremely, but I have yet to win Anjelica with my newfound wealth."

"Just don't take too long. My aunt and uncle are liable to make things pretty hot for me."

"Don't worry. I'm on the hunt. Good luck, Old Boy."

He lurked around the side of the house and Bentley headed the other way with the bags. I breathed deeply, choked on a passing ash cloud and admired the lake at the foot of the hill. Dankworth Hall was on the opposite shore of Lake Sputum to my own estate. In the distance one could make out the tiny town of Catarrh, with its fertilizer plant merrily belching smoke.

I approached the morning room with some trepidation. My Aunt Hypatia was warlike at the best of times and the rumor that I had frittered away the family fortune was apt to bring out the Mongol horde in her.

As I opened the door, I observed my aunt gazing out of the window with an expression that on any other human face I would have described as "happy." She held a long-stemmed rose which she mashed against her nose as she inhaled its bouquet. She turned to see me cowering at the door and a smile broke out on her face as if she had spotted an approaching ice cream truck.

"Cyril! Darling! Live free or die."

I frowned at her. "Hello, Aunt. Live free or die. Are you quite well?"

"Never better. Why are you hunched over in the corner? Come, let me look at you."

I inched tentatively toward her in case this was a ruse to bring me within biting distance. "Look here, Aunt, I'm a bit confused."

"About what?"

"Aren't you furious with me?"

"What on earth for? Oh, you mean because you've lost all your money. But what is money?"

I stared at her. "Well, if you don't know I certainly haven't a clue."

She waved the rose in her hand cheerfully. "Anjelica has explained it all to me. You see, it is not money which makes one rich. Being wealthy is a state of mind."

"Really?"

"You must feel, deep in your core, that rich is what you are. If you *identify* as rich, you *are* rich, and people must treat you as such."

I wrestled with this concept. "Even if you're poor?"

She smiled at me indulgently. "You cannot be both rich and poor simultaneously. That would be middle class—a fate I would not wish on my worst enemies."

"Well, that's a relief. I thought you'd be angry."

"I am never angry. I am passionate. That is another thing Anjelica has shown me. Apparently, it all stems from a disconnect between my ego and my id, whatever those are. Have you met Anjelica yet?"

"No. Looking forward to it terribly."

"I believe she is in the library with her followers. Let me introduce you to her."

My Aunt Hypatia took me by the hand. To the best of my recollection this was the first time we had made physical contact. Her hand was warm and dry, like the belly of an iguana that had been sunning itself on a rock. She led me to the library.

"There you are, Anjelica. Oh, hello, Cheswick. Live free or die."

"Hallo, Hypatia. Live free or die."

Binky stood holding the hand of a young lady. As she turned, I was struck by the size and luminescence of her eyes. I couldn't shake the memory of a picture in one of my children's books of something that was once called a lemur. She was a tiny thing and one instantly felt that one would hurl oneself into traffic to protect her. Scattered around her on the floor was a band of saffron-clad individuals with blissful looks on their faces. She spoke in a thrillingly mellow voice.

"Hello, dear Hypatia."

"Anjelica, I would like you to meet my nephew, Cyril Chippington-Smythe. Cyril, this is Ms. Anjelica De Souza-Kleinhoffer."

"Deucedly glad to meet you. Binky here has told me scads about you."

She turned to Binky accusingly. "Has he? That was very naughty of him. We are all part of the universal whole, after all. There is nothing so special about me that I am worth discussing."

Her followers were unable to contain their enthusiasm. They broke off from chanting and began murmuring among themselves.

"Isn't she wonderful?!"

"We love you, Mistress!"

Anjelica silenced them with a look. "Hush now."

They fell back on their haunches and prepared to confront the infinite again.

"Sorry, Mistress."

"We'll meditate harder. We promise."

My aunt regarded them with amusement. She leaned toward me conspiratorially. "I do not choose to meditate, but if I did, I would win easily."

Binky was looking down at his shoes with a blush on his cheeks. "I'm awfully sorry for talking about you, dear Anjelica."

She playfully struck him on the arm. "Instead of talking about me, you should have been telling him about the work. Did you urge him to join us?"

He brightened at once. "Oh, yes! Of course I did. Cyril, didn't I tell you about Anjelica's work?"

His offstage eye blinked at me madly and I did the decent thing.

"Oh, yes. Talked of nothing else. Damned persuasive he was."

"What did he tell you, exactly?"

This brought me up short. "Oh. Well... you know, about the work... and those who strive to carry on... the work... and all that."

"And do you wish to join us?"

"Well... I would, of course, but as I'm sure Binky told you I am absolutely destitute and must spend every waking moment trying to keep body and soul together. Blame Croesus here—it was he who put me in this precarious position while becoming unimaginably wealthy himself."

She whirled around to stare at Binky. "Wealthy? Cheswick! When were you going to tell me?"

"I was just about to."

"You are rich?"

"I am. Simply drenched in the stuff."

Binky's plan seemed to be working like gangbusters. Anjelica gazed at him worshipfully.

"But that's wonderful! Now you can fund our project."

The room, which had been bright with sunlight, suddenly darkened. The air thickened.

"What?" I choked.

Binky too, had gone rather still. "What?"

"Your riches will make the world a better place—a more equitable place. Think how many of the poor we can elevate with all of that money."

I was sure I must have misheard her. "All?!"

She smiled at me. "To keep it would be unethical when so many live in despair."

"Of course, a small donation is called for," I stammered, "But let's not over-achieve."

"I see you are concerned for your friend's well-being, but do not worry. I myself gave away my entire fortune and I have never been more at peace. There is nothing so destructive as riches."

Binky grew thoughtful. "You know, Cyril, you said much the same thing not long ago."

I glared at him. "That was hypothetical, which means it was a lie."

Anjelica suddenly drew near to me and turned the lamps of her eyes on mine. The room began to swim. "Poor thing. You are new to penury. It will grow easier. I will help you. Together we shall toil among the masses and you will see that nothing is deadlier to the human spirit than great wealth."

I found myself saying, "Shall we? Jolly good. Sooner the better."

Aunt Hypatia clapped her hands gaily. "You see, Cyril? Already she has done what I could not despite years of ultimatums. She has found some good in you."

Anjelica continued massaging my forearm.

Binky was staring daggers at me. "My angel, didn't you express a desire to explore the forest behind the house? Come, I'll escort you."

"Of course. Everyone, keep chanting until I return."

Her followers picked up the pace and began rocking and chanting at a furious pace.

"Until later, Mr. Chippington-Smythe?"

With those enormous headlights shining in my eyes the best I could come up with was, "Er...yes."

Anjelica and Binky swept out the French doors and disappeared around the corner. My aunt watched them go with evident satisfaction.

"There, what did I say? A remarkable young lady."

"Indeed, Aunt. But what was all that about the money?"

She grimaced. "I do not think about money. It gives a sharpness to one's features. But here is your uncle. He thinks of nothing else, as his hatchet-like profile can attest."

My Uncle Hugo stepped through the door. He glared at the saffron-robed acolytes. "Drat! It's like living in a pipe organ."

"Hugo, here is your nephew."

"I see you were able to cancel your other engagements."

"Of course! Wild houses couldn't have kept me away."

He squinted at me. "I believe you mean horses."

"Sorry, what?"

"Horses. They were... oh, never mind. Damn the Great Extinction."

My aunt clucked her tongue and Uncle Hugo subsided.

"Cyril wants to know about Anjelica's financial dealings."

He grunted. "Nonsense if you ask me—giving all your money to the poor. What does that accomplish but to add one more to their number? There are simply too many of them for even the greatest fortune to make a difference."

"Have you donated to the cause?"

"Not likely."

"You, Aunt?"

My uncle smiled grimly. "Your aunt has no access to our accounts. I made sure of that."

"He thinks himself very clever, but I have all of the benefits of wealth and none of the worries, so who's the Sly Boots, him or me?"

"You, Aunt, always. No one would dispute it."

My uncle eyed me grimly. "Where do things stand with you and the club?"

"I am persona non grata. Alas."

"I shall speak to them on Monday. This cannot continue, even if I have to stand guarantor for your debts myself."

"Uncle! I am moved beyond measure."

"You can repay me out of your wages."

There was a sudden tightness in my chest. "My what?"

"I shall start you in my office at the lowest level of employment possible. You will begin by sweeping up and gradually work yourself into a more elevated position."

"But I've never worked a day in my life!"

"You should have thought of that before you began wagering on the relative speed of vermin."

This called for action! "Look here, I can't explain... honour seals my lips, but there have been some misapprehensions concerning the financial dealings between Binky and myself that I hope to clear up in the near future."

Uncle Hugo was unmoved. "That's as may be. Until then you'll show up at my office on Monday prepared to wield a push broom. We open at eight."

The blood rushed from my head. I grew dizzy. "That's practically the middle of the night!"

"If you are not there I shall come to your home and pull you out of bed by the nose. Is that clear?"

Capitulation was inevitable. "Yes, Uncle."

My aunt gave a satisfied nod. "There, I told you your uncle could explain everything. I must speak to the auto-cooker about lunch."

"I wish you'd let me find you a real cook. Mine has changed my life."

"You alarm me. Change is a terrifying thing. Once we accept the possibility of change, we are thrown into a whirlwind of chaos and existential angst. And for what... some soup? No thank you."

"Fine."

She patted my hand. "Cheeseworth is joining us for lunch. That should cheer you up."

"He's always good for a laugh."

"Why not take a stroll until the warning cannon?"

"Thanks Aunt. Perhaps I'll catch up to Binky and Anjelica."

The forest behind Dankworth Hall is practically primeval. Binky and Anjelica were nowhere in sight. I chose a path at random and in no time was hopelessly lost.

I found a stick and whacked at the underbrush, which cheered me up for a while, but finally I grew despondent and sat on a rock waiting to be rescued. After a moment I thought I could make out voices nearby, so I marshaled my reserves and staggered toward them.

Upon reaching the edge of a clearing I was startled to see Cheeseworth standing before a colourful pavilion directing Alice and Pansy Witherspoon (née Freehold) as they attempted to build a campfire. I noted that matrimony had not made Alice's teeth any smaller. If anything, marital bliss had made them more prominent. Cheeseworth shooed them away from the fire pit.

"Don't pack the wood so tightly. You'll smother the flames. Kindling first, then larger twigs and we'll add the logs once the smaller pieces have caught."

His affectations seemed to have fallen away—the eccentric speech impediments, the flowery verbiage. Was it all a counterfeit? I stepped into the clearing and the three woodland nymphs started as if I had caught them planning a heist.

"Hallo! This is a pastoral tableau," I said suspiciously.

Alice raised a piece of kindling like an Amazonian warrior. "Cyril! How dare you spy on us from the bushes? You are no gentleman."

Pansy smiled at me cheerfully. "Hello, Cyril. Live free or die."

"Yes. Live free and all that."

I caught a sudden movement out of the corner of my eye and turned to see Compton, Cheeseworth's pet sheep, pretending to graze on a nearby shrub. His fleecy coat was full of twigs and burrs and he looked absolutely miserable.

"Ah, Compton, you're here too."

"Yes, Sir. Baaa. How pleasant to see you again. You don't have anything edible about you, do you? These leaves play havoc with one's stomach."

"Sorry, no. The life of a pet is a perilous one, I find."

"It is not for the faint of heart, Sir. Baa."

Cheeseworth had been staring at me nervously. He licked his lips and assumed an artful pose. "What a wovely surpwise, dear boy! How long have you been there in the underbwush?"

"Only a few moments. I say, just now you seemed... what I mean to say is... you sounded rather different just now."

He waved away my suspicions. "What? Widiculous! It must be the wustic acoustics of the fowest."

"I could have sworn..."

"Oh leave it alone, Cyril, for heaven's sake," Alice snapped. "Be a mensch."

"What are you doing camping out in the middle of my aunt's property? Is this part of the honeymoon?"

Pansy laughed. "Goodness no. We spent our honeymoon in Venice. It was glorious."

"Ah. Did you tour the Piazza San Marco?"

"Yes, with scuba gear. All the little shops are still intact under the lagoon. We returned a week ago and came to stay with Hypatia while our flat's being painted."

"But why this primitive abode?"

Alice spoke through gritted teeth. "We couldn't bear all that chanting at the house. Like living in a hive of mechanical bees."

"Are you joining us for lunch?"

"Of course."

Compton looked up hopefully. "Am I invited?"

Cheeseworth picked up a thin branch and whacked Compton on the fleecy back a few times.

"Of course not. Bad sheep! No animals in the house. You stay here and guard the tent."

"Yes, Sir. Baaa."

There was a distant boom. Alice began straightening her clothing. "There's the first cannon."

"Binky's here too."

She snorted. "That simpleton?"

Pansy poked Alice with a twig. "Alice, be nice."

"Sorry, my love. I'm trying."

"I suppose you know Ms. De Souza-Kleinhoffer?"

"Know her? I went to school with her. Conceited little simp."

"Alice," Pansy chided.

"Sorry, but she is. Always going on about the poor. She couldn't care less about the poor."

I frowned. "I'm sure she does. She gave away her fortune, after all."

Alice fixed me with a scornful look. "She never had a fortune. Her father lost everything betting on soybean futures."

I stared at her. "But her work with the less fortunate..."

"She's never met a poor person in her life. She just wants everyone to think she's a saint."

"I'm sure you're wrong."

Cheeseworth shook his head sadly. "She's not, you know. She asked me for a donation and I looked into her charity. It does absolutely nothing."

"What does she do with all the money she raises?"

"Spends it, I suppose."

I considered for a moment. "I should tell Binky. He's besotted with her."

Alice snorted. "Oh she'd never go for him. He's too poor."

A horrible premonition stole over me. "Ah. I feel there is something you should know."

And with that I confessed everything: the *ruse de guerre*; Binky's false wealth; my supposed ruin. They listened with mouths agape and eyes agog.

When I had finished, Alice was the first to react. "You really are an idiot."

"Alice," said Pansy reproachfully.

"Well, isn't he?"

"He's trying to help a friend."

As Alice considered the situation, a smile slowly grew on her face. This had the unfortunate side effect of exposing her teeth. I looked away.

"Binky and Anjelica. It would serve the two of them right if they got married. How I'd laugh! Look here, we should try to help them along."

"What fun," chortled Cheeseworth. "They can have the wedding at Cheeseworth House and the honeymoon in the poorhouse."

This seemed a little cold to me. "I don't know if I can let my friend be practiced upon like this."

Alice poked a bony finger into my chest. "If you say a word, Cyril, I'll tell the whole world about your escapade in the Netherlands."

"You wouldn't!"

Pansy looked at us curiously. "What happened in the Netherlands?"

"Nothing," I said hurriedly. "It was a youthful indiscretion involving a biplane and a breached dike."

Alice snorted. "It forced the relocation of The Hague, that's all."

"You swore you'd never tell."

"Just keep mum and follow our lead."

There was another boom in the distance.

"Second cannon. We'll have to hurry."

Cheeseworth looked about him. "Let me get my monocle and walking stick. I'm simply slavering with anticipation."

Well, there I was on the horns of a dilemma without a paddle. My best friend was in the clutches of an adventuress and if I lifted a finger to warn him, I would soon be in the clutches of the Dutch authorities. It would take a Machiavelli of the first order to find a way through this maze and Bentley was having a fit of temperament to equal any soprano you care to name. I girded my loins for what was certain to be an epic battle of wills and led our ragged little band toward the looming battlements of Dankworth House, where plots and counterplots seethed and roiled like the odious depths of Lake Sputum.

CHAPTER FOUR

Be Careful What You Wish For

As I quickly changed for lunch, I studiously avoided eye contact with Bentley. He had failed to be useful and I intended that he should suffer. He seemed oblivious to my coldness, but I knew that he missed nothing. I reached for my favourite tie and he could stay silent no longer.

"Not that tie, Sir."

"What's wrong with it?"

"The juxtaposition of ducks and balloons is a touch too jocular for the occasion, Sir."

I looked at him frostily. "I disagree. The tie is *comme il faut*."

"Very well, Sir, but may I suggest that wearing it with the Scotch plaid vest diminishes both tie and vest."

He seemed determined not to feel my disapproval and I knew that my endurance was no match for his.

"Look here, Bentley, this can't go on."

"What can't go on, Sir?"

"This lack of assistance in a crisis."

"I hardly think the vest constitutes a crisis."

"It's not about the vest!"

He gave a little sniff. "I am sorry if I have not given satisfaction. Shall I order a replacement for myself?"

"Don't be ridiculous. I don't want a new valet, I want you to step up and lend a hand."

"If Sir would communicate what is needed, I shall endeavour to be useful."

So, I told him about Anjelica's mendacity and Alice's plot, leaving nothing out. He regarded me gravely.

"A precarious position, if I may say so."

"We're teetering on a knife's edge."

"Is that all of it, Sir?"

"Isn't that enough?"

He stood for a moment and I could hear the gears in his head grinding away merrily. After a long pause he jerked back into motion and stepped toward the door.

"If Sir has finished dressing, I must attend to one or two matters."

I eyed him closely. He seemed to me to be the Bentley of old. The ice had not exactly thawed, but at least there was a hint of condensation. "Of course! Off you go."

As soon as he left the room, I ripped off the Scotch plaid vest. We may have been locked in a battle for moral supremacy but no one has ever questioned Bentley's fashion sense.

I skipped down the stairs and spotted Bentley bending Binky's ear at the entrance to the dining room. He passed him an envelope and shimmered away. This was my chance to put a friend on his guard, Alice or no Alice. I jogged up to Binky and gave his arm a brief pummeling. "What ho, Old Misery. I've got to speak to you privately."

"Of course. What is it"?

My aunt's voice blared from the dining room.

"Cyril! Cheswick! Don't linger in the doorway. Everyone is waiting."

I faced the dining room and saw that all eyes were staring in our direction, including the somewhat bloodshot pair belonging to Alice. I shrugged and led Binky over the threshold. "I'll catch you up later," I murmured in his ear. "Sorry, Aunt. Hallo, Everyone! Sorry we're late. Live free or die."

"Live free or die."

"Live free or die."

"Live free or die."

"Live free or die."

"Live fwee or die."

"Live free or die," declaimed my aunt, "And that, I believe, completes the festivities. Pine, you may serve."

"Yes, Ma'am."

Pine bobbed a curtsy and exited the dining room. Alice flashed her teeth in a wolfish kind of way and leaned across the table. "How lovely to see you again, Anjelica."

"And you as well. It has been many years since our carefree schoolgirl days. I'm sure we are quite different people now."

"Oh, I don't know. Do people really change?"

Aunt Hypatia examined her spoon and reached for a napkin. "No, thank goodness! It is quite hard enough to judge people once. Imagine having to constantly revise one's opinion."

Anjelica looked at her reprovingly. "Of course, people can change. I, for example, was a horrible child—selfish, vain. I hope that I have grown kinder with time."

My aunt was unconvinced. "Time rarely improves anything. The only exceptions are wine and memories of puberty."

Anjelica shook her head. "I disagree. You, for example, Hypatia, have grown more self-actualized and integrated in the short time I have known you. Your list of 'I wants' has shrunk precipitously as your 'I needs' have grown."

"You've been a good influence on me, my dear."

I timidly raised a hand. "Sorry, I believe you lapsed into a foreign language I am unfamiliar with."

"Anjelica has developed a system," said Binky proudly.

"I have merely extended the theories of minds far greater than my own."

"It works a treat," chuckled my aunt. "She had me crying like a child. Most invigorating."

I was trying to picture my aunt feeling emotion of any kind.

"You must tell us all the details," Alice exclaimed breathlessly. "I'm positively perspiring to know more."

My aunt wrinkled her forehead thoughtfully. "It's all about how one takes things, or some such.

For example, if I tell Cyril here that he is a vile chancre sore on the lip of society..."

"Oh, I say!"

" ...His habitual response would be to sulk. But what if he could control his response so that if I called him an infected abscess on the family backside..."

"Well, really!"

"...Instead of being hurt he reacted with pleasure and satisfaction? Would his life not be infinitely better?"

Anjelica smiled upon my aunt like the prize student she was. "Exactly! It's about having new responses to old stimuli."

Binky turned to examine me. "Does it only work with words? What if I slapped Cyril in the face?"

Anjelica nodded encouragingly. "He can choose to respond to that stimulus with pain or with pleasure. It is his choice."

Binky slid his chair back a bit. "Let's try it!"

"You do and I'll bite you."

He lowered his hand. "Spoilsport."

Anjelica closed her eyes and gave a little bow of the head. "We are each responsible for our own happiness. If we are unhappy, we have no one to blame but ourselves."

My aunt looked doubtful. "I have not yet accepted that Hugo is free of blame, but it's early days."

Mrs. Pine clumped into the dining room carrying a flimsy piece of paper. "Pardon me, Ma'am, a semaphore come just now."

"Yes? What does it say?"

She peered at the paper. "'Jepson's Crisps—same great taste, half the polysaccharides. Try our newest flavour: sea salt and ash.'"

"Is that all?"

"Yes, Ma'am."

My aunt waved Mrs. Pine away and she clumped back toward the kitchen.

I looked around. "I say, where are your followers, Anjelica?"

My aunt tut-tutted. "Oh, they do not dine with us. They eat a sort of bland paste in the gazebo."

"Flavour of any kind would be too distracting," Anjelica explained. "As they evolve, we will reintroduce flavours like bitter and sour and so on."

Alice put down her glass and smiled innocently. "So... I hear there's a little romance going on between you and Cheswick, Anjelica."

Binky turned a rosy hue and stared down at his plate. "Oh, I say..."

Anjelica was unperturbed. "I am not embarrassed to admit that we feel an attraction for each other."

Binky turned to her and a look of astonishment emerged on his face like a bubble rising from a pot of oatmeal. "Do we? Oh, darling..."

My aunt was quick to intervene. "Not at table, Cheswick. Love and good digestion rarely coexist."

"I am the happiest of men!"

"Well done, you," exclaimed Alice. "And you've had a stroke of good fortune? Refilled the family coffers I understand?"

Binky glanced at me. "Yes. I don't like to talk about it in front of Cyril, he being destitute and all."

Pansy looked over sympathetically. "Oh, Cyril, how awful."

"Yes. Well, *que sera, sera*."

Cheeseworth looked up sharply. "I know that one. It's something to do with cheese."

"You mustn't pity me. All is not as black as it appears. I wouldn't be surprised to find myself back on top very soon."

Pansy beamed at me encouragingly. "That's right, Cyril. You mustn't give up hope. Be brave."

My uncle harrumphed. "If you believe janitorial work will make you rich you are sadly misinformed."

The door swung open and Mrs. Pine rolled a squeaky serving cart covered with plates into the room. My aunt peered at it.

"Ah, the first course. It looks like chickeny nuggets, although the sauce is mysterious. Wine sauce is seldom such a vibrant yellow."

Mrs. Pine ducked a little curtsy. "Auto-cooker dumped in the whole bottle of curry powder, Ma'am."

My aunt's face fell. "Did it? Oh well."

I gazed sadly at the mustard-coloured lumps. "You really could be eating so much better, Aunt."

"No, thank you. Food should be treated like an unruly child: held down until it is subdued."

I shrugged. "You can lend a horse some water..."

My uncle sat up and stared at me. "I beg your pardon?"

"Isn't that a saying?"

"I am not overly familiar with what used to be called horses, but I don't believe they purchased water on credit."

"My mistake. Tell us more about your charity, Anjelica. Specifically, whom have you helped... and please name names?"

"Oh, countless people."

"And you've given them money? That can be traced?"

"Yes, we give them money, but that isn't really the point. After all, no matter how much we give, we only relieve their suffering for a day, a week, a month. The problems of the poor are systemic."

"That sounds contagious," my aunt observed nervously.

"Our work isn't only about the less fortunate. The real purpose of our charity is to eliminate the corrosive effects of wealth."

Uncle Hugo looked deeply offended. "You speak of wealth as a plague. Wealth is a blessing."

Anjelica regarded him doubtfully. "Is it? You are wealthy, Hugo, but if you will forgive me for saying so, you don't seem happy."

"Happiness is only found in fairy tales."

Anjelica shook her head. "No. It is attainable by anyone, but you must be brave enough to seize it. Look at Alice and Pansy. They saw their happiness in each other and they grasped it. You are happy, are you not?"

Pansy smiled shyly at Alice. "Oh yes. Ecstatic."

"I must confess, our lives are rather blissful."

"Whereas you, Hugo, toil at a job you do not enjoy to produce more money than you could ever spend, the fruits of which bring you no pleasure."

"That is called being a responsible adult."

"Then I shall remain a child."

My aunt clapped her hands. "Bravo, my dear. A hit. A palpable hit."

Anjelica leaned in. "You are trapped by the expectations of others. I doubt you have any idea what the inner Hugo really wants anymore."

My Uncle stared at his plate gloomily. "At the moment I would settle for something edible."

Now she swung her attention to me. "What about you, Cyril? Binky told me of the misery your wealth had brought you. Can you deny that the wager that cost you your fortune removed a terrible burden from you?"

I goggled at her. "I say, you should work in a carnival reading minds."

Binky looked confused. "But I love being rich."

She patted his hand indulgently. "No. You feel the flush of excitement at the change in your circumstances. Soon the sweetness of your wealth will pall and you will long for your old life of simple pleasures. But I will save you. You shall not be crucified on a cross of gold while I draw breath."

Cheeseworth looked up and adjusted his monocle. "A stwiking turn of phwase."

Binky seized Anjelica's hand. "My angel! You will save me! I am yours!"

Alice clapped her hands gaily. "Beautifully said, Cheswick. I think you and Anjelica make a lovely couple. Pansy and I are very happy for you."

"Yes indeed," Pansy murmured.

"When's the wedding?"

I almost jumped out of my chair. "Alice! Don't embarrass them!"

Binky peeked at Anjelica shyly from under his lashes. "Well, you know, I haven't asked her yet."

Alice clucked her tongue disapprovingly. "You haven't? What are you waiting for?"

"Now, let's not pressure the lovebirds!" I practically shouted. "These things take time!"

"Nonsense. Faint heart never won fair lady. We could all be dead tomorrow."

My aunt turned to her in alarm. "Why? What have you heard?"

"I think you should get down on your knee right this minute and propose."

Sweat was pouring off of me. My brain raced. "Not in those pants! You'll ruin the crease. I say, Pine, is Bentley anywhere about?"

"I haven't seen him, Sir."

Alice impaled me with a glare. "Now, Cyril, the *dike* of Cheswick's emotions is beginning to crack. Don't stick your thumb in like the little *Dutch* boy or you'll be sorry."

Cheeseworth jiggled in his chair. "What a colourful extended metaphor. This is a conversation wife with litewary devices."

Binky took a deep breath and rose to his feet. The luncheon guests froze. "Anjelica! May I speak to you alone?"

"Before pudding?" my aunt clucked. "How precipitate!"

Anjelica rose demurely. "Of course, Cheswick."

"Excuse us, everyone."

And with that, the poor sap led Anjelica from the room like the condemned man cheerfully leading the hangman to the gallows. As the door closed behind them Alice gave a little "whoop!"

"That's done it! They're as good as married."

I jumped to my feet. "Pardon me for a moment. I must find Bentley."

"No, you don't. Sit back down. You're not going to spoil the game."

"But look here..."

"Sit! Unless you have a passion for windmills."

"Oh... really!"

My aunt looked somewhat lost. "Why this censure of windmills? I have always found them charming... although in a high wind the enthusiasm of their motion can be rather agitating. Ah! The pudding. I hope the auto-cooker has not taken any liberties with it." She peered at the serving cart that Mrs. Pine was rolling toward her. "No, it looks quite inoffensive. Would anyone care for custard sauce on their Spotted Dick?"

I may come to a boil slowly, but once heated I must act. I pushed back my chair with my delicious Spotted Dick half eaten and faced Alice across the table.

"Look here, Binky is my boon companion and I won't allow him to be cozened into a match that will ruin him. Flagellate me with tulips if you must, but I'm going to save my friend."

Alice gave a dismissive wave. "Goodness. I didn't know you were so passionate. Very well, we've had our fun. Run to the rescue."

"Do hurry, Cyril," Pansy quavered. "Suddenly I feel terribly guilty."

As I headed for the door, I heard my aunt continuing to spoon pudding into bowls. "I confess I am in the dark on the matter of tulip flagellation. Is this a fad?"

"If it is not, I shall make it one," cackled Cheeseworth.

As I raced through the halls, Binky and Anjelica were nowhere in sight. I ran to my room—no Bentley. I raced to the servant's hall—no Bentley. Finally, almost fainting with exhaustion, I spotted him walking through the front door.

"Bentley! Where on earth have you been?"

"It was necessary to send several semaphores, Sir."

"Semaphores at a time like this! The game is afoot! Binky is proposing to Anjelica at this very moment."

"Yes, Sir. I anticipated the event. I thought it best not to interfere at this juncture."

"But once she says 'yes' he's a dead duck. How could you let this happen?"

"When a young man is in love, he is deaf to reason, Sir. We require unassailable proof of Ms. De Souza-Kleinhoffer's perfidy if we are to turn him from the path of his own destruction."

I looked at him closely. "And you have such proof?"

"I am in the process of acquiring it. I am sorry to observe, Sir, that you have a rather large smear of spotted dick on the tie you are so fond of."

"To Hades with the tie. This whole weekend is a disaster."

"Surely not. Lake Sputum looks most inviting. Shall I lay out your wet suit and respirator?"

I drew myself up. "With my friend in danger? For shame."

"As you wish. If there is nothing else, there are things I must attend to."

"You may go."

I moped back to the dining room, hoping to spot the unlucky couple while there was still time, but as I entered the room from one end, the door opposite me opened and Binky practically floated in on a cloud. Anjelica paced shyly next to him, the roses in her cheeks giving witness to the tender scene that had just occurred.

"Congratulate us, everyone. We're engaged!"

Alice raised her glass. "Three cheers for the bride and groom. Hip hip..."

"Hooray!"

"Hip hip..."

"Hooray!"

"Hip hip..."

"Hooray!"

Anjelica took Binky's hand in a firm grip. "Thank you all. We are very fortunate."

As the celebration began to subside, Binky sidled over and murmured in my ear, "This is all your doing, Old Chum. I shall never forget it."

"That's what I'm afraid of. Look here, I've got to talk to you. Can we slip out for a moment?"

"Anjelica, my love, may I step into the hall with Cyril for a tick?"

"Of course, my darling. I must compose telegrams to my family and friends. Please excuse me everyone."

She glided out one door and Binky and I headed for the other. My aunt sniffed. "This luncheon has taken on a rather Bohemian flavour. Don't people linger over coffee anymore?"

Cheeseworth stared greedily at the cups. "I love coffee. Is it weal?"

"Practically. Hugo has a mysterious source but I believe the concoction is more than half sphagnum moss."

The rest of the conversation was inaudible as we closed the door behind us.

"Thank you awfully, Cyril. This is all your doing."

"Stop saying that. It will haunt me to my grave."

"What do you mean?"

"We've been bamboozled by an adventuress."

"Sorry, what?"

"Anjelica is not what she seems."

He gazed at me anxiously. "A woman?"

"Of course she's a woman."

"Thank goodness! You gave me quite a start."

I took him by the shoulders and gave him a shake. "She didn't give her fortune to the poor. Her father frittered it away on soybeans."

Binky whistled. "He must have an unnatural affection for the stuff."

"Betting on soybean futures! Stop interrupting."

"Sorry. Go on."

"Her charity is a sham. It hasn't spent a penny on the poor. She's only marrying you because she thinks you're rich."

"How can you know all this?"

"Alice told me. She went to school with her."

"She's jealous! She resents the transfer of my affections from her to Anjelica."

"Don't be absurd. She's very happy with Pansy. She doesn't give a fig for your affections."

"Why are you trying to ruin this? I thought you were my friend."

"I am. Look here, what do you think is going to happen when she finds out you lied to her?"

"About what?"

"About being rich."

"Oh. Well, couldn't I go on pretending?"

I stared at him. "With what money?"

"Yours. You've got plenty after all."

"I have no intention of subsidizing the rest of your life with that false prophetess. You are hereby cut off."

He seemed unable to meet my eyes. His fingers twitched nervously. "Oh dear, there may be some slight problem."

"What might that be?"

"Well, you know how these things go... there I was and there she was, and I'd proposed and she'd just said yes. I was rather giddy with happiness... and when she asked for a little donation to her charity naturally I couldn't say no."

"How much?"

"Hmmm? What?"

"How much did you give her?"

His eyes darted around the hallway. "I really couldn't say."

"What do you mean you couldn't say?"

"Well... she suggested that I leave the amount blank until she talked to her board members to see what the tax implications were and all that."

I was seized with a horrible realization. "You gave her a blank check?"

"Well... yes."

"Drawn on my account at the club?"

He was shrinking before my eyes. "Mmm hmmm."

"She could write a cheque for my entire fortune!"

"Why would she do that?"

"Because she's a criminal!"

"Says who?"

"I do!"

He patted my hand, which was wrapped around his tie and was slowly cutting off his air supply. I loosened my grip.

"Don't panic," he wheezed. "I have an infallible instinct about people. I know in my heart that Anjelica is good."

"I am happy to listen to arguments on both sides once that cheque is destroyed."

"She can't do anything with it here in the country. I'll get it from her before we leave."

I saw a sudden movement out of the window and glanced down at the lawn. "Hallo! What's this?"

It was Anjelica. She was practically running toward the lake. "Where do you suppose she's off to?"

"She said she might take the boat for a spin."

"Odd." Suddenly I froze. "Hang on, is there a bank in Catarrh?"

"I presume so."

I jumped like I'd been bitten. "Great Zeus! She's going to cash that check!"

And with that, Binky fainted dead away. I stared at him, then out of the window. This was a moment of crisis and we Chippington-Smythes have always known what to do in a crisis.

"Bentley! I need you! Come at once! Help!"

CHAPTER FIVE

Showdown on Lake Sputum

There are moments in life that define one's character. When faced with a crisis, some panic and run aimlessly about the room with arms flapping; some become bloodthirsty tyrants who impose their will on all and sundry and some are wise enough to know when to delegate authority. I am such a delegator and Bentley is invariably the delegatee. He took in the scene at once: Binky out cold; Anjelica racing to the only available watercraft with a cheque that could ruin me clutched in her delicate hands and the Catarrh National Bank just across the water.

"We're in the soup, Bentley!"

"Do not despair, Sir. The situation is not as bleak as you suppose. I suggest that we decamp to the lakefront."

At that moment Binky regained consciousness. He looked around groggily. "What... where... Anjelica! Where is she?"

"Headed for the boat, cheque in hand."

He scrambled to his feet. "We've got to stop her!"

Bentley gave a little bow. "Fear not, Sir..."

The rest of his thought was lost as Binky pounded away down the hallway. "Follow me! I know what to do," he called out over his shoulder.

Bentley gave a little sigh. "His response was peremptory. If he had allowed me..."

"No time, Bentley! We've got to follow him before he does something stupid!"

I raced down the hall in pursuit with Bentley behind me. We found Binky in the driveway climbing into his motorized swan boat.

"Get in! We can catch her!"

I stared at the enormous swan, which had lost a good deal of plumage on the drive down and now looked down at me with sad resignation.

"In this monstrosity?"

"It's amphibious."

"Oh! Jolly good. Come on, Bentley."

I climbed in the front and Bentley bestowed himself in the back. At that moment Cheeseworth ambled around the corner of the house leading Compton by a string around his neck.

"Hallo! Where are you chaps wunning off to?"

"Anjelica is absconding with the family fortune. We are in pursuit!"

"I say! Swide over. Compton, you can crouch on the floor."

Compton, who had hopped eagerly into the back seat, crawled sadly down onto the floor and wedged himself between Cheeseworth's feet with a dispirited bleat.

My aunt made her appearance. "What is the meaning of this caravansary?"

"We're in pursuit of a cwiminal mastermind," chortled Cheeseworth.

"Indeed? Hugo! Come at once!"

My uncle, with his suspenders down, peered suspiciously out of the doorway. "I was about to take my nap."

"Your siesta can wait. Get into the car. I shall explain to you as soon as I understand it myself. It is fortunate that you brought such a capacious vehicle, Cheswick."

"I suppose it's useless to protest," my uncle grumbled.

"It is."

Alice and Pansy came strolling across the lawn, hand in hand. Upon seeing us all disposing ourselves in the car, they trotted over.

"Where are we all going?"

"Just get in!"

"I love a mystery," said Pansy.

Binky was bouncing up and down behind the wheel. "Hurry up, for God's sake! She's getting away!"

Bentley leaned forward from the rear of the swan. "There really is no need..."

"No time! Off we go!"

We raced across the lawn toward the lake. I could see that Anjelica had unmoored the boat and was heading into open water.

"Hang on!" cried Binky.

We hit the water at high speed and skated thirty feet into the lake before the motor sputtered and died. There was an eerie stillness. Finally, my aunt looked around.

"Is this part of the plan?"

Binky looked puzzled. "The motor stopped. I don't understand."

I looked at him with a dawning suspicion. "Are you sure this vehicle is amphibious?"

"Well it's a bloody swan, isn't it? Swans are sea fowl, aren't they?"

"It's a car in the shape of a swan. That doesn't ensure that it swims. Did they specifically tell you it was amphibious?"

"Well... no."

There was a brief pause as we all digested this information.

Alice turned to Pansy. "This seems about the sort of adventure one would expect with Cheswick behind the wheel. I'm sorry I got you into this, my love."

"I'm not at all disappointed. I can't wait to see what happens next."

My aunt peered across the lake. "Ah, there is Anjelica. I'm glad she is taking some time to enjoy herself. Yoo-hoo!"

I watched the distance between us widen. "She's enjoying herself entirely too much. She's getting away!"

"What do you mean, getting away?"

Binky was twiddling knobs and mashing on pedals. "She's trying to steal Cyril's fortune."

"Didn't you already do that?"

I fell back into my seat with a sigh. "I think it's time we came clean, Old Fish."

I explained the situation in as few words as possible, from our true financial positions to Anjelica's attempted larceny.

My aunt gazed out over the water as she listened. "It beggars belief, but nowadays it seems the more improbable a scheme is, the more people will subscribe to it. That is true of politics, at any rate." She peered at Anjelica in the distance. "There must be some credible explanation. I could not be so mistaken about a person."

Just then Anjelica raised her thumb to her tiny nose and gave us a loud raspberry. She waved the hand with the cheque in it at us, then balanced herself in the boat and shook her derriere at us. "Nya nya nya! Nya nya nya!"

My aunt frowned. "That was surprising."

"So long, suckers! See you in the funny papers."

The colour drained from Binky's cheeks. "She's... she's a monster!"

"You're well out of it, Cheswick," Alice clucked sympathetically. "Imagine if you'd married her."

"You're right. I know you're right."

Uncle Hugo could stand no more. He extended his arm out of the window and shook his fist at the departing skiff. "You will be hearing from my solicitors, young lady," He turned to my aunt. "Are we just going to sit here and watch her escape?"

"Sit still, Hugo. Take a nap."

When all other possibilities have been exhausted there is still one place a chap can turn. "Well, Bentley? Any ideas?"

"Yes, Sir. I believe you will find that all will end to your satisfaction."

"How can that be? Our relative positions widen by the second."

"The race is not always to the swift. Observe."

I squinted across the water and noticed that Anjelica was displaying signs of distress. She stood uncertainly, gazing down at the bottom of the boat—which seemed, to my eyes at least, as if it sat lower in the water than it was wont to do. "I say! Is she sinking?"

"Oh, the poor thing!" exclaimed Pansy.

Bentley watched Anjelica's struggles impassively. "I took the liberty of drilling several holes in the bottom of the boat, Sir. I suspected that Ms. De Souza-Kleinhoffer might attempt to flee."

"Why didn't you tell us?"

He looked at me dryly. "I did attempt..."

"See here," my uncle interrupted, "We're still trapped in the middle of this stew of a lake with no way to reach the shore."

Bentley gave a little bow. "The water is not terribly deep, Sir. I shall simply carry you across one at a time."

That's Bentley—an answer for everything.

"And what of Anjelica?"

"She must swim. I shall ready a course of antibiotics. I think I can promise that the cheque will not survive immersion in this acidic medium."

There was something rather horrible about watching Anjelica slipping inexorably under the malodorous solution that filled the lake. The last thing to submerge was the check. It hovered in the air, clutched in her tiny hand until it too sank under the oily surface. There were some moments of suspense and then her head emerged and she began the long dog paddle to shore. We made the trip in comfort, safe in the powerful arms of Bentley who deposited us safe and dry on the dock. Compton was the last to be rescued. He kicked up his heels and gamboled a bit. Bentley made sure we were all intact and faced me.

"I shall just put my garments to soak before they are eaten away, Sir."

"Yes, of course. We shall stay to confront Anjelica."

"She should be put under a hot shower and scrubbed with a powerful detergent as soon as possible."

"First the scolding, then the scalding."

He gave me an approving look. "Very good, Sir."

Bentley glided toward the house and we watched the sodden mass that was Anjelica hoist itself onto the dock. Her saffron-robed followers had gathered on the shore and stood staring at her. My aunt stood forth.

"What have you to say for yourself, young lady?"

To Anjelica's credit, she didn't give up. Even with the rapidly dissolving cheque turning to pulp in her hands she faced my aunt with her chin up. "Dear Hypatia, I know you are feeling something that unevolved people call 'betrayal,' but this is an illusion. You can apply new ways of responding to old stimuli. I will help you."

My aunt held up a hand. "What is that phrase the young people are using? Oh yes... stuff it!"

Anjelica finally gave up the fight. Her face transformed from a placid smile to a spiteful grimace. "Rats!"

My aunt jumped and looked around her. "Where?"

"I give up. Go soak your head, you old battle-ax."

Uncle Hugo sputtered, "See here..."

"Be quiet, Hugo. I am quite capable of speaking for myself."

"I mean, really."

Anjelica plopped down on the dock and scratched her head vigorously. "I know I'm blown up. Just call the police and get it over with."

My aunt waved dismissively. "Police? Who said anything about police?"

"I'm a fraud. My charity is nonexistent." She jerked her thumb at Binky. "I tried to rob this feather-headed nitwit of everything he had."

"Ha! It wasn't my money, it was Cyril's, so who's the feather-headed nitwit now?"

"Still you, Old Boy," I observed.

"Oh. Damn."

My aunt considered. "You did not succeed, so I see no need for the police and the news services that follow in their wake. You must leave my house. That is the chief thing."

"And stop taking donations to that phony charity," added Alice.

"How do you expect me to live?"

Cheeseworth twirled his monocle thoughtfully. "It stwikes me that you have all the tools necessary to be a theatrical producer. You have a gift for convincing people to give you money while offering them little hope of ever getting it back. I know several people in the entertainment industry. I shall contact them on your behalf."

She looked up at him gratefully. "I say, that's pretty square of you."

Compton, who was following this part of the conversation closely, sidled up to Anjelica. He produced a rather wrinkled photograph from inside his fleece. "Could I just slip you my pic and resume? Don't judge by my current employment. I stood by for the lead in 'Lilac Time' last season and went on twice."

Anjelica wearily grabbed the picture and Compton slunk away.

"And what have you to say to me?" sniffed Binky.

"Well, obviously the wedding is off."

"Obviously."

"What else is there to say?"

"Some might think an apology is in order."

"Yes. Sorry."

Alice snorted. "A little thin. You did break his heart, after all."

Anjelica climbed to her feet and faced Binky. "Look here, I made it clear I intended to take all your money for the foundation, didn't I?"

"Well, yes," he stammered.

"And you still wanted to marry me?"

"Of course."

"Then you went into this with your eyes open. The only difference is that instead of spending your money on the poor I was going to spend it on me."

An expression very like hope kindled on his simple, pudding-like face. "You mean, you still want to get married?"

She gazed at him speculatively. "Do you have any money at all?"

"Not really."

"Then no. Sorry."

My aunt grunted her assent. "Your answer is quite sensible. A man without money is like a cheap novel—amusing but ultimately disappointing."

Anjelica finally noticed her followers standing in a confused clump. "What are you all waiting for? Get lost. It's over."

They stared at her, then at each other. Finally, one timid acolyte raised his hand. "Is this a test?"

Anjelica stared at him. "A test?"

"To see how strong our faith is?"

"No. I really am a fraud."

Her followers murmured amongst themselves for a moment and another of their number stepped forth.

"But that's what you'd say if you were testing us."

Anjelica exhaled noisily. "I'm not testing you!"

They assembled again and there was some back and forth.

"We don't believe you."

"We won't abandon you."

Anjelica looked at them with a mixture of disgust and calculation. "Oh for the love of... fine! It was a test and you all passed. Does anyone have a car?"

A tiny follower timidly raised a finger. "I do."

"You can drive us all back to town. I've got to get out of these things. My skin is beginning to burn."

"Bentley's warming up the shower for you with a scrub brush and some lye soap."

"You'll probably lose your hair," observed Alice, "But it will grow back."

Anjelica started to trudge toward the house, then stopped and turned back to us. "I suppose I should thank you for letting me go."

"If it was up to me..." began my uncle.

"But fortunately, it is not," observed my aunt. "Indeed, there is little in our daily life that requires your input. Weren't you complaining about your lack of a siesta? Go and lie down at once."

"Yes dear."

Uncle Hugo followed Anjelica toward the back door. Cheeseworth smoothed his jacket and inserted his monocle.

"If you'll excuse me, I must enter today's events in my diary while they are fwesh. Thank you for a memorable weekend, Hypatia."

"I meant for it to be completely forgettable but fate had other plans."

This felt like my cue to depart. "Well, I've had enough of the country for one lifetime. Binky, are you coming?"

"I've got to have this swan boat towed out and disinfected."

"Then I'll see you back in town. Thanks awfully for the weekend, Aunt. Could Pine call for a car?"

Ensconced in the passenger seat of a painfully plain rental car I stared at the back of Bentley's stately head. "I say, Bentley..."

"Sir?"

"Did you take note of all that stuff Anjelica was spouting about each of us being responsible for our own happiness?"

"I did."

"It's got me thinking. I know she was only an adventuress, but was she on to something?"

"No, Sir. That is an age-old bit of flim-flam used by charlatans of every type. They endeavour to convince their followers that if they are unhappy, it is because of some defect in their own character. The charlatan is then free to abuse them in every possible way and their poor followers blame themselves for feeling abused."

"Diabolical."

"Indeed, Sir."

"Where do you suppose Binky got hold of one of my cheque books? I never gave him one."

"I gave it to him, Sir, as he was entering the dining room for lunch."

"Why the dickens did you do that?"

"I assumed that Ms. De Souza-Kleinhoffer would importune him for a contribution. I gave him the means to comply, hoping that when the opportunity to become rich presented itself she would reveal her true nature."

"Brilliant! Hannibal and his elephants are nothing to you."

"Very gratifying, Sir."

"And what were those semaphores you sent?"

"One was to Evans at the club, instructing him to cancel the arrangement you made concerning Mr. Wickford-Davies's access to your account."

"That was quick thinking. So even if Anjelica had reached Catarrh, she wouldn't have been able to cash the check."

"No, Sir."

"What other stratagems did you employ?"

"I contacted your lawyer and your accountant, Sir. I instructed them to create a new trust for you."

I looked at him in surprise. "Are you empowered to act on my behalf to such an extent?"

"Yes, Sir. I have had your power of attorney since you were nine. Your parents thought it prudent."

"And what is the nature of this trust?"

"It will contain all of your possessions. The trustees, which include myself and your uncle, will manage your businesses and the trust will pay you an allowance each month sufficient to pay your living expenses."

A dawning comprehension stirred in the old noodle. "But no more?"

"No, Sir. You will have to live somewhat more frugally, but not painfully so."

"Heaven! And you've made sure I can't touch the bulk of my riches under any circumstances?"

"I have made certain of it, Sir. My memory banks contain the contents of several respected law libraries."

I leaned back into the soft, luxurious Naugahyde. "Oh! Bentley! I feel like a new man! I'm free!"

He glanced at me in the rear-view mirror. "I'm glad you are pleased, Sir."

A wave of gratitude rose up within me. "I don't know what to say."

"No words are needed, Sir. If you are satisfied that is enough."

I leaned forward. "No... No, it's not enough. Bentley..."

"Sir?"

"Please be so good as to return the TV."

There was a brief moment of silence before he replied. "Thank you, Sir. As it happens, I placed a file inside one of the bread rolls. By now they should have cut through the chains and made good their escape. I do appreciate the gesture. Shall we go in?"

I looked up to see the welcome sight of my own front door. I stepped across the threshold and listened to the beautiful silence of an empty house.

"It's wonderful!"

He set the bags down in the front hall.

"Let's get you out of your traveling clothes and I'll bring you a brandy and something pharmaceutical."

As I sat before the hydrogen fire in my pajamas enjoying the effects of brandy and Prozac, I reflected on the vagaries of fortune that lift some men up and cast others down.

"I say, Bentley, do you ever wonder what life would be like without money?"

"The possibility could not arise, since no one without money could afford to employ a servant of my nature, Sir."

"True. I'd be alone, then. Poor, friendless, reduced to selling my organs or some such desperate occupation. How is it that a mere accident of birth could make all the difference?"

"It is the way of the world, Sir."

"But should it be so?"

"I merely observe that is has always been so, and therefore this system must be deeply rooted in the most basic urges of humanity. If change is to come, it must come from those with the power and the resources to effect it."

I turned to look at him. "And who is that?"

"You, Sir."

"Oh, right." I watched the flames dancing in the grate. "It's a lot to take in. Perhaps tomorrow I can set aside some time to exercise the old brain cells. Remind me, will you?"

"Of course. Will there be anything else? I plan on changing my oil this evening if you have no further need of me."

"No. Off you go. I'll put myself to bed."

I watched Bentley glide away with a feeling of deep contentment. I made a solemn resolution that I would behave sensibly from now on. I would devote my life to self-improvement and I would start by cutting back on the old alcohol. I flipped the rest of my brandy toward the fireplace... and that is when the fire started.

But that is another tale.

The End

If you enjoyed this book, please
take a moment to visit
Amazon and provide a short
review; every reader's voice is

extremely important for the life
of a book or series.

If you'd like advance notice on the next book's
release head to:
WWW.TwitsChronicles.com
where you can sign up for my email list and where
you can ask Cyril and his friends a question which
they may choose to answer in a newsletter.
I hate spam as much as you do, so I will keep
emails to a minimum.

**Cyril, Bentley and The Usual Suspects will
return in:**

TWITS ON THE HUNT

The next installment of THE TWITS
CHRONICLES.

Read on for a taste:

Time, it has always seemed to me, is not the linear inflexible creature that we are taught to believe in. It has a taffy-like quality that can stretch endlessly on a Sunday afternoon. On this particular Sunday it had clearly lost all motivation and flopped around the house sighing and flipping through old magazines with a woeful expression, so it was a positive relief when Bentley wafted in on a breeze to inform me that my chinless cousin, Cheswick Wickford-Davies (Binky, to his friends) was in the front hallway doing something odd.

Bentley, as I'm sure you are aware, is my mechanical valet. His origins are shrouded in the mists of antiquity but he's been with the family for generations and his loyalty and resourcefulness are beyond question.

"What do you mean, odd? Odder than usual?"

"I would describe his manner as furtive, Sir. He is standing by a window and peeping through the curtains."

"Better see what it's about, then."

I trundled off to the front hallway, where I found Binky engaged in the aforementioned peeping. He was crouched next to a preserved walrus that had been harpooned by my great-great grandfather, Percy. Alas, this proud pinniped would never have a mate stuffed and mounted by his side. Since The Great Extinction, walruses had joined the rhinoceros and the zebu in that great menagerie in the sky.

I peered over his shoulder to see what he was staring at. "Hallo, Old Boot! What's it all about?"

He shrieked and leaped into the air. Holding a hand to his heart he stared at me and slid slowly down the wall to sit on the marble tiles. He pantomimed for me to hang on for a tick and laboured to slow his breathing. Bentley and I watched him carefully.

"Shall I fetch my medical kit, Sir?"

I leaned over and shouted in Binky's ear. "Do you want some drugs, Old sot?"

He shook his head and made a superhuman effort to speak. "No! No, I'm all right. Just let me sit here for a moment."

"Sorry if I startled you."

"It wasn't your fault. I'm a bit on edge."

"So I see. Live free or die."

"Live free or die. Could you take a peek out front and see if there's anyone lurking about?"

"Only too glad." I parted the curtains and gave the street the once over. "Nothing untoward that I can see. Just a young person cleaning her nails with a knife."

"What? Help me up!"

"She can't be more than ten! You're not frightened of a child!"

"That's why she's so dangerous! No one would suspect her. Give me a hand, will you?"

I hauled him onto his trotters and brushed him down in a general way. He peered out of the window.

"Diabolical," he muttered.

I looked at Bentley inquiringly.

"I believe Mr. Wickford-Davies's apprehension stems from a debt of honor. Isn't that right, Sir?"

"What? Oh, yes, a debt of honour without question. It was a sure thing, you know."

I patted him gently on the soft part of his head. "I'm not sure you understand what that phrase actually means, Old Clot."

He slumped. "I've landed myself in the frying pan for good this time and no onions to soften the fall."

I turned to Bentley. "Can you shed some light?"

"According to my sources, Mr. Wickford-Davies made a rather substantial wager on the outcome of the Annual Delivery Persons' Race."

Binky stared at Bentley in awe but I was used to this omniscience that he trotted out when called upon. The Annual Delivery Persons' Race, for those who have not had the pleasure, is a fete organized by my club, "Twits." Any member of the Delivery Persons Union is eligible. They race around an obstacle course with their delivery carts and the winner receives a trophy which is engraved with their name and displayed in a glass case near the club cloakroom. It is not uncommon for large wagers to be placed on the favorites.

"I couldn't lose! Ernie could give the rest of the field twenty yards and still breeze home by a length."

"Ernie? My Head of Research?"

"He still moonlights at his delivery job. Says it offers more opportunity for advancement than scientific exploration."

"All right, you bet on him and presumably he lost?"

"He was nobbled! Someone loosened the wheels on his cart. They fell off halfway down the course. Even so, he came in second."

"And now you owe money to a shady criminal enterprise?"

"Of course not! The betting for these things is controlled by the government—Bureau of Wagers. Nothing shady about it."

"Then who is following you?"

"Bureau of Collections. Bunch of fanatics. Chop off your thumbs as soon as look at you."

"These hooligans work for the government?"

"Absolutely. Civil Service. Pension, benefits... it's a plum job."

"This is ridiculous. How much do you owe them? I'll cover it."

"You will? Bless you, Old Friend."

"Can't have them chopping off your thumbs, what? How would you play bridge?"

"I could be the dummy."

Before I could choose a punchline, Bentley cleared his throat. "Forgive me, Sir, but if my information is correct, you do not have sufficient funds to cover the amount in question."

I stared at him. "How can that be? I'm as rich as Midas."

"You are forgetting that you are on an allowance. The bulk of your wealth is beyond your reach."

"When did that happen?"

"It was a recent occurrence. If you recall, you felt that endless riches leached all the flavour from life. You wished to be relieved of that burden and the solution was to put you on a strict allowance."

I looked at Binky sharply. "How could you bet such an enormous sum?"

"It was a sure thing."

"Stop saying that. Why would they allow you to make such a bet? It must be pretty generally known that you're a sponger of the first water."

He blushed and looked nervously at his toes. "Oh dear, you're going to be cross with me."

"Will I?"

"Yes. You see, I may have put you down as a co-signer on the bet."

"And they took your word?"

"Not exactly. I may have... forged your signature just a teensy bit."

I stared at him in shock. "You did what?"

"It was nothing! You would never have known about it."

"Do you mean I'm on the hook for your losses?"

"I was going to cut you in on the winnings. It was a sure..."

"If you say that again I swear I'll pull you by the nose."

He fell silent and looked at me gloomily. I set to work assimilating all this info into the old gray matter but odd bits kept sliding out of the frame. Finally, I turned to Bentley.

"I'm stumped, Bentley. Should we hand him over to the authorities?"

He gave a little shake of the head. "I'm afraid Mr. Wickford-Davies would not thrive in a prison environment. Perhaps we can find a solution if given a bit of time."

There was a knock on the door. We all stared at it apprehensively.

"What should we do?" I whispered to Bentley. He stepped up to the door and looked through the peephole. A harsh voice spoke from outside.

"I see the shadow on the other side of the peephole. I know you are at home. My name is Mr. Null. I am from the government. I must ask you to open the door."

TWITS was originally produced and distributed by Dori Berinstein, Alan Seales and the Broadway Podcast Network - the premier digital storytelling destination for everyone, everywhere who loves theatre and the performing arts. BPN.fm/Twits

About The Author

Born in Canton Ohio and raised in a box made out of ticky-tacky, Tom Alan Robbins spent his youth as a middle-aged character actor. He has appeared in nine Broadway shows, including *The Lion King* in which he created the role of Pumbaa. He recently received a Grammy nomination for the cast album of *Little Shop of Horrors*. He has maintained a parallel career as a writer, penning scripts for TV shows like *Coach* and writing plays, one of which (*Muse*) recently won the New Works of Merit Playwriting Competition.

The Twits Chronicles series is his first attempt at novel writing and it has been a pure joy. He hopes to keep creating adventures for Cyril and

Bentley as long as there are readers who enjoy them.

Also By Tom Alan Robbins